Frederick

Leo Lionni

Andersen Press

All along the meadow where the cows grazed and the horses ran, there was an old stone wall.

In that wall, not far from the barn and the granary, a chatty family of field mice had their home.

But the farmers had moved away, the barn was abandoned, and the granary stood empty. And since winter was not far off, the little mice began to gather corn and nuts and wheat and straw. They all worked day and night.

All – except Frederick.

"Frederick, why don't you work?" they asked.
"I do work," said Frederick. "I gather sun rays
for the cold dark winter days."

And when they saw Frederick sitting there, staring at the meadow, they said, "And now, Frederick?"
"I gather colours," answered Frederick simply. "For winter is grey."

And once Frederick seemed half asleep. "Are you dreaming, Frederick?" they asked reproachfully.

But Frederick said, "Oh no, I am gathering words.
For the winter days are long and many, and we'll
run out of things to say."

The winter days came, and when the first snow fell the five little field mice took to their hideout in the stones.

In the beginning there was lots to eat, and the mice told stories of foolish foxes and silly cats. They were a happy family.

But little by little they had nibbled
up most of the nuts and berries,
the straw was gone, and the
corn was only a memory.
It was cold in the wall
and no one felt like
chatting.

Then they remembered what Frederick
had said about sun rays and colours
and words. "What about your
supplies, Frederick?"
they asked.

"Close your eyes," said Frederick, as he climbed on a big stone. "Now I send you the rays of the sun. Do you feel how their golden glow . . ." And as Frederick spoke of the sun the four little mice began to feel warmer.

Was it Frederick's voice?
Was it magic?

"And how about the colours, Frederick?" they asked anxiously. "Close your eyes again," Frederick said. And when he told them of the blue periwinkles, the red poppies in the yellow wheat, and the green leaves of the berry bush, they saw the colours as clearly as if they had been painted in their minds.

"And the words, Frederick?"

Frederick cleared his throat, waited
a moment, and then, as if from
a stage, he said:

"Who scatters snowflakes? Who melts the ice?
Who spoils the weather? Who makes it nice?
Who grows the four-leaf clovers in June?
Who dims the daylight? Who lights the moon?

Four little field mice who live in the sky.
Four little field mice . . . like you and I.

One is the Springmouse who turns on the showers.
Then comes the Summer who paints in the flowers.
The Fallmouse is next with walnuts and wheat.
And Winter is last . . . with little cold feet.

Aren't we lucky the seasons are four?
Think of a year with one less . . . or one more!"

When Frederick had finished, they all applauded.
"But Frederick," they said, "you are a poet!"

Frederick blushed, took a bow, and said shyly, "I know it."